Evil's Last Look

Book Three
The Stories of Jo

Açil Pichon

Edited by Sharon Slavinsky & Ricky Graves
Graphic Design by Julian Graves
Cover Design by Debbi Stocco

Printed in the United States of America
First Printing, 2017
ISBN: 978-0-9987736-7-4 (print)

Açil Pichon Publishing
Louisiana
www.acilpichon.com

For mothers who have done their best,
but live with regret.

God My Father,
You are my direction, light, and strength.
Thank you for your many blessings, and I know
I am here for you.

Contents

One

Half

When Jo's ex-husband CJ realized that Jo would never be with him again, he threatened to take Jo to court to fight her for half of her interior design firm's business. Jo was shocked when she received papers from a lawyer hired by CJ, because she knew CJ wasn't smart enough to come up with that idea on his own. After Jo was served with those papers, she called CJ to find out what was going on.

"I received papers from a lawyer today saying you want half of my business," said Jo to CJ during the phone conversation.

"Yeah," replied CJ. "What's wrong with that?"

"You didn't help me start that business," said Jo.

"We was married when you got that business, so half is mine," said CJ.

"Bullshit! You got the house and don't pay one dollar in child support," said Jo angrily. "That's already more than you deserve."

"See ya in court," said CJ.

At the beginning of that phone conversation, Jo was furious, but once she settled down and got a level head, she contacted her lawyer.

"Jo, how's business going right now?" asked her attorney Mr. Tucker.

"Business hasn't been doing very well," said Jo. "With the economy the way it is, businesses aren't building or opening new locations, and people aren't renovating."

"From what I remember, CJ doesn't pay you any child support, right? Or Does he?" asked Mr. Tucker.

"No, he doesn't. He doesn't pay for anything the girls need. Plus I've been paying our oldest daughter Isabella's full college tuition," answered Jo.

"Have you been keeping good expense records for your business?" asked Mr. Tucker.

"Yes, you know I do," said Jo.

"Great! Stop by my office one day this week and bring your books," Mr. Tucker said. "Don't worry about making an appointment, because I have an open schedule this week."

"I'll see you tomorrow then," said Jo.

The following day, Jo met with Mr. Tucker, and after going over her business expenses, she had no more worries about CJ getting half. The books indicated that business had been in the red for quite some time. There was no profit. All Jo could do was laugh as she told Mr. Tucker, "I don't have a problem giving CJ half of nothing."

Mr. Tucker joined Jo in laughter, and once they stopped laughing, they proceeded with business. Jo and Mr. Tucker both decided it was best to end Jo's Interior Design Firm business after legal proceedings were finalized with CJ and his lawyer. When CJ found out he was getting nothing, he called Jo full of anger.

"What the fuck them lawyers talkin bout you ain't got no money?" he yelled.

"Not that it's any of your business, but most of my money goes toward health and life insurances for the girls, and Isabella's college tuition, which you don't contribute a penny to," said Jo. "It seems you too stupid to know that raising daughters cost money, plus business hasn't been good."

"I know you got money, Bitch," yelled CJ.

"Ok CJ, but I tell you what. Keep messing with me and I will be taking YOU to court for back child support," said Jo.

CJ had no comeback for that. He was speechless, and hung up.

After Jo made that threat, she received several anonymous text messages containing verbal and physical threats. When Jo notified the authorities about the threatening messages, they were eventually traced back to Candy and CJ's older sister's cellphones.

Two

Loss

After settling and closing all business accounts for Jo's Interior Design Firm, Jo went back to work in the office at UPS. About a year after Jo returned to UPS, her mother's cancer came back more aggressively than before. When the doctors noticed, the cancer had spread to other parts of her body, and there wasn't much they could do, other than help keep her comfortable. Even though Jo's mother knew she was dying, she refused hospice care.

Every spare moment Jo had, she was at her parents' house assisting them as much as they'd allow her to. Jo spent as much time as she could with her mother. Unfortunately, Jo's mom had more bad days than good, and caring for her was emotionally hard on Jo. To see her once extremely independent mother in such a frail and helpless state tore Jo up on the inside. Many times Jo had to walk out of the room to hide tears from her mother.

As Jo cared for her mom, she did so in such a way not to cause her mother to lose dignity. Lacking knowledge where healthcare was concerned, Jo took things a day a time, and did the best she could. When she struggled more than usual, or had additional questions about home healthcare needs, she turned to her best friend Carmen. The one person she called Sista. Most times when Jo opened up to Carmen, she broke down in tears because she felt so helpless.

"I am having a hard time bathing Mom," Jo said to Carmen. "She is very weak, and getting her in and out of the tub is hard."

"Your mom is a small woman. She can't be that heavy," said Carmen.

"No. But I'm still having trouble lifting her. My legs and arms have been hurting," said Jo. "I guess it's all the extra lifting I've been doing, topped with the fact that I am worn out."

"Jo, you need to take care of yourself. And why don't you have a shower seat for your mom to use?" asked Carmen.

"I didn't think of that, and I'm not sure how to get one. Plus, Mom has refused hospice services. Don't they usually provide things like that?" asked Jo.

"Fuck that!" said Carmen. "Do you have that paper that the hospice lady gave to you when you were at the hospital the last time? Or do you have her phone number?" Carmen asked.

7

Jo found hospice's telephone number and gave it to Carmen. Within minutes, Carmen arranged for not only a shower chair to be delivered to Jo's parents' house, but a walker and a hospital bed too. Unfortunately, Jo's mother didn't live much longer after she started receiving hospice care. She went to be with the Lord towards the end of that summer.

To family members, Jo appeared to be strong when her mother passed away.

"Jo is taking things quite well," her dad would say to his sisters. "She's strong."

In reality, Jo was falling apart on the inside, while fighting to keep it together for everyone else. Her dad needed her to help him take care of their business affairs and make funeral arrangements. Plus, Jo's daughters were having a hard time with their grandmother's death, so Jo needed to be strong for them as well.

After the funeral services were over, everyone went back to their regular routines. Jo kept quite busy, which helped to keep her mind off of missing her mother. That was until she'd go over to visit her dad and see he was mourning himself to death.

One evening Jo stopped by to check on her dad like she always did every evening. When she walked in the door, there he sat in his favorite spot on the sofa. His legs were crossed like always, and his right arm resting on his side with a beer in his hand.

"Dad," Jo said as she walked over to him. "Dad," she said again when she bent down and kissed his cold and stiff forehead.

Realizing her dad was gone, Jo sat to gather herself.

"Less than a year ago, I sat next to my mother like this," thought Jo. "What do I do now?"

Jo did the one thing she always did every time she found herself in a dark situation. She called Carmen. Carmen was at Jo's parents' house in no time, and she took the bull by the horn like always. Carmen handled everything. Even things Jo didn't think of. Carmen made all necessary phone calls and arrangements, and she directed Jo to where she needed to be, when she needed to be there, to do what she needed to do.

After losing both parents, and dealing with Psycho's internet harassments, Jo had a hard time with life. She felt evil was attacking her from every direction, and no matter where she turned, it was around every corner waiting for her.

Jo always loathed living in Mississippi, so being there multiplied her problems by ten. Since her parents were gone, her daughters were grown, and there was nothing else holding her back in miserable Mississippi as she called it, she thought it was the perfect time for her to move away from there.

Once that thought entered her mind, she did not hesitate to plan accordingly. Jo put a transfer request in at UPS, and as soon as that request went through, she packed her belongings, hired a property manager to put her parents' house up for rent, purchased a quaint cottage on the beach, and moved to the sunshine state.

Away from small town gossip and bad memories, Jo strived to find peace.

Three

Repast

After about two months, Jo was completely settled in her beach cottage in Florida. She worked five, sometimes six days a week, and that was the only time she was around other people. When Jo left work each day, she was completely alone and felt a sense of uneasiness. Many times Jo didn't know what to do with herself, because for the first time in over twenty years, she did not have anyone to take care of or look after. In addition to learning how to be alone with herself, she was still dealing with the loss of her parents, and was still disturbed by the internet harassments and threats she'd received from Psycho. On top of all that, CJ was still a thorn in her side. Even though he was parading all around Mississippi and Louisiana with Candy at his side, he still called Jo every chance he got and when she least expected it. CJ apologized to Jo ten times over, and continued to beg her to take him back.

"We didn't make it in Miser cuz of the people. Ya know how my people is. They don't wanna see nobody happy," said CJ. "Let me come to Florida by you," he continued to beg.

When Jo's parents passed away, she treated CJ like family. Jo allowed him to be around her family during preparations, ride in the family car with her, and sit with her and the girls in the church during the funeral service. CJ sat next to Jo during everything like a proud peacock. He just knew he had his foot back in the door.

"My sistas say they hope you not mad with them," said CJ.

"Your people are what they are. Not worthy of my anger. I'm not mad. Just smarter," said Jo. "They're your people, not mine, and I don't have to deal with them."

"They wanna be here fa you. You not gonna get mad huh?" asked CJ.

Besides welcoming and allowing CJ to be around her during those hard times, she didn't say anything when his low down mother and sisters called and came around too. The unforgiving and untrusting part of her wanted to tell them to get the hell away, which she should've done, but the forgiving and peaceful side of her just let the devils be. She knew they weren't there because they cared about her or her family. They were only there to do what they always did. Looking for any reason to gather, drink, and party; even an after funeral repast.

"CJ, the less I think about your people, the better I am," said Jo. "So please, let me be."

Not thinking about or dealing with CJ's people is exactly what Jo did. When she saw them at the funeral, she looked through them. Jo saw them for what they really were; Devils looking for attention and self-gratification. As no surprise, one of CJ's sisters started a rumor about Jo's younger daughter Jaylynn.

At the repast, the news came out that Jaylynn was leaving to go out of state for college. When CJ's older sister Pam heard that, she took that little piece of information and ran all around Miser gossiping.

"Jaylynn pregnant," Pam told every and anybody in Miser who knew Jaylynn. "I know she going outa state cuz she pregnant."

To make her gossip seem like a concern, she sent Jaylynn a letter.

"You're not the first person this happened to, and you won't be the last," Pam wrote in the letter to Jaylynn.

When Jaylynn got that letter from Pam, she was so upset, and she called her mom fussing and cursing.

"Mom, I hate them people," said Jaylynn.

"What now honey?" asked Jo.

"That bitch Pam sent me a letter talking about I'm pregnant," Jaylynn snapped.

"Watch your mouth girl," said Jo. "Read the letter to me."

"I'll scan it and send it to you so you can read it yourself," said Jaylynn. "My daddy's people make me sick!"

Jaylynn had just begun her first year of college out of state at the time, and she was doing quite well. She was still a virgin, so being accused of being pregnant sent her over the roof.

16

"I got away from there because I want to better myself. I don't want to end up like them. They too dumb and stupid to even know something is wrong with em," said Jaylynn.

"Honey, just do what you have to do there in Colorado and don't worry about anyone in Mississippi," said Jo. "Next time you get a letter from her, don't even open it. Tear it up and throw it away. You don't need any negativity in your life right now, or ever for that matter; especially from ignorant people like them."

"Mom, I never want to see them people again. I hope they all die," said Jaylynn.

"That's not nice Jaylynn," said Jo. "You should never wish anything bad on anyone. Not even them. No matter how horrible they are."

Four
One out of Two

Jo didn't like when Jaylynn was upset; especially about something pertaining to CJ or his family members.

Most phone calls from Jaylynn brought a little excitement to Jo's life. She could sit and listen to Jaylynn on the phone for hours talking about her college life. Jaylynn had a lot of stories to tell. She'd tell good and bad stories about her classes, professors, dates she'd been on, guys she'd met, friends she was hanging out with, and even parties she'd attended. Hearing Jaylynn's college stories brought back a lot of good memories. It made her think about her old college days.

"Life was so simple back then," thought Jo.

Preaching to or teaching Jaylynn is something Jo did every chance she got, because she didn't want Jaylynn to make the same mistakes she'd made, or the same mistakes her older sister Isabella was making at the time. Jo did everything she could do in order to protect Jaylynn from the same evils that crossed her path throughout life. Most times Jaylynn listened to her mother, but other times, just like most teenagers, Jaylynn thought she knew everything, and her mother knew nothing.

"Mom, you're preaching to me again," Jaylynn would say.

Raising children was something Jo found to be the biggest challenge in her life. No matter how much CJ and others told her she was a great mother, she still felt like she failed as a mother; especially where her older daughter Isabella was concerned.

For many reasons, Isabella had grown to be a huge disappointment, but like always Jo blamed herself for Isabella's shortcomings.

"If I would've moved and taken my children away from CJ and his family when they were younger, they wouldn't be the way that they are today," Jo once said to her mother.

Sometimes when Jo sat with her mother, she'd think about all the mistakes and bad choices she'd made where CJ was concerned. Speaking with a lot of regret in her voice, she'd say, "I knew what those people were about. I should've known better not to expose my children to them. But nooooo! I wanted to keep my family together. I was too busy worrying about giving CJ what he wanted that I neglected to do what was best for my children. I should've done like the wives and husbands of all the other men and women in CJ's family did.

As soon as they knew without a shadow of a doubt what kind of family they married into, they took their kids and left," said Jo. "They got as far away from them crazy ass people as they could. Unlike me, they had enough sense and courage to leave."

Jo had so much bitterness for CJ at that time, and every time he called her on the phone, she didn't hesitate to give him a piece of her mind.

"What's happened to us Jo?" CJ always asked.

"If you were in the same marriage that I was in, you would know that you weren't just a shitty ass husband," said Jo. "You were a horrible ass daddy too."

Even though Jo blamed herself for exposing her kids to CJ and his family's way of life, she also blamed CJ for not protecting her or their kids from their destructive ways.

"A real man protects his family CJ," said Jo. "You never protected the girls or me. You let your people do and say all kinds of things to the girls and me."

"I know! I'm sorry I didn't do right by ya'll," said CJ. "I know I ain't a good daddy to them girls. Stop blaming yo-self for the way things is. You were. No. You ARE a good momma. Always been. Don't let nobody tell you different."

CJ always said the right things when he was trying to get Jo back.

"And don't worry about Isabella," said CJ. "I will get her ass in line. I know she the way she is cuz-a me."

Isabella failed out of college after her first year, and moved back in with her dad. A friend of CJ's hired Isabella to work as a salesperson at his tree farm, but she didn't go to work most days. The only thing mattered to Isabella was getting high. She smoked weed morning, noon, night, and in between. She was once a very beautiful girl; extremely attractive to most. She went from looking like a runway model to looking like a dirty flower child or hippy. Isabella quit getting her hair trimmed and fixed nicely. Instead, she allowed her hair to grow out, and it looked matted together and unclean. Similar to dreadlocks, but much worse.

Whenever Jo visited Miser, she looked forward to seeing and spending a little time with Isabella, but the stench in her clothes, skin, and hair made Jo sick to the stomach. The one defining moment that multiplied Jo's disappointment in Isabella was when she found out Isabella was five months pregnant by an abusive boyfriend

Every time Jo thought about the hard life Isabella was making for herself, she preached that much more to her younger daughter Jaylynn.

"Keep up with your grades Jaylynn," Jo would say.

"I will Mom," replied Jaylynn. "I am not going to do like Isabella,"

"God knows how much I love you and your sister, and I pray every day for you two to have an easier path in life than the one I chose," said Jo. "Seeing your sister the way she is breaks my heart. Please don't make the same mistakes."

"I'll never be like Isabella Mom," Jaylynn replied. "You DON'T have THAT to worry about."

"Thank you Honey," said Jo. "Make God, yourself, and me proud."

Five

Demons and Crabs

In Florida, there were many large
condominiums coming up along the beach, and
Jo saw that as an open opportunity to get a few
interior design jobs, which was her passion and
work of choice.

Jo's impressive portfolio and five star
customer reviews contributed toward her getting
the bid on one of the two condominium design
contracts she placed. Even though she would be
working for herself again, she decided it was
best to keep her office job at UPS. The work

she did was not strenuous or too time consuming, and the benefits were great.

Working for UPS thirty-five hours a week and for herself in her spare time kept Jo very busy. The busier Jo stayed the better, because when she did slow down, it was hard to keep overpowering memories of past and present demons out of her mind.

After going through a divorce, losing both her parents, worrying about Isabella, being harassed and threatened by a psychotic ex-boyfriend, dealing with the trauma of seeing that psycho killed right in front of her face was taking a toll on Jo. Prayer and meditation were the only things that brought some sense of comfort and peace to her life.

One night just as Jo sat down in bed with a book to read, her cell phone rang. She picked up the phone, looked at the number calling, she didn't recognize the number, so she put the phone back down on the nightstand and didn't bother to answer.

"If it's important, they'll leave a message," thought Jo, as she went back to reading the book.

Jo's cellphone made a sound just as it did when someone left a voicemail. Jo put the book back down, picked up the phone, and listened to the voice message.

"Hello Jo, this is your cousin Tamara. I know I am the last person you want to hear from, but I need to talk to you. Please call me as soon as you get this message. It's about Isabella," said Tamara.

Tamara definitely was one of the last people Jo wanted to hear from. For years, Tamara was the one and only person Jo confided in until she learned that Tamara was the one telling all of her business to family members and strangers around Miser.

For years Tamara smiled in Jo's face, and acted like she was her best friend, which was far from the truth. Tamara was the type of person Jo called a crab. A crab in a bucket. As soon as one crab started to climb out of the bucket, Tamara would do or say anything to pull them back down.

Reluctantly, Jo called Tamara back.

"Tamara. I got your message. What's going on?" asked Jo, quickly and straight to the point.

"I saw CJ older sister, Pam. She was blasting Isabella and you," Tamara said.

"Blasting? What do you mean by blasting?" Jo asked.

"TALKING BAD about y'all. She say Isabella is big and pregnant, about to deliver, homeless, strung out on drugs," said Tamara. "She say you ain't no kinda momma to have your daughter out on them streets like that."

"Isabella is grown, and she's made choices in her life that she has to live with. As for being homeless, she was living with her daddy," said Jo. "Plus I don't even live in Mississippi anymore."

"I know. That's what I told that bitch Pam," said Tamara. "I told her you didn't live there anymore. I see them Sims still no good. She supposed to be the aunt. Why can't she help? Why they blaming you and not CJ sorry ass?"

"Thank you for letting me know about Isabella," said Jo. "If you find out anything else, please let me know."

"I will," said Tamara.

"Thanks," replied Jo with appreciation.

Six

World's Best Dad

Jo arranged to take a few days off of work and drove west to Mississippi to see if she could find Isabella. On her drive there, she called Jaylynn to see if she knew anything.

"Jaylynn, have you heard from your sister lately?" asked Jo.

"No mom. I tried calling her one night, but her phone was disconnected," said Jaylynn. "Is everything alright Mom?"

"We're talking about your sister Isabella, so no. From what I hear, things are not alright," said Jo concerned.

After striking out with Jaylynn, Jo decided to call CJ to see what he knew.

"What is going on with Isabella?" Jo asked CJ. "Your sister is running her big sloppy ass all around Miser talking bad about Isabella. She says Isabella is strung out on the streets, homeless, and about to deliver that baby any moment. What is going on? I thought Isabella was living with you. You said you were going to get her together."

"I can't do nothin with that girl," said CJ in a defensive tone. "Bella was here with me, but she left one day and didn't come back."

"Why did she leave?" asked Jo.

"I don't know. You know how that girl is. She gotta bad attitude an you can't tell ha nothin," answered CJ.

"What were you trying to tell her that made her leave? Were you two arguing or something?" asked Jo.

"Isabella like ta argue. So yeah! She got flip with me an I tode ha ass to get out," said CJ.

"I know Isabella is argumentative, but to put your eight month pregnant daughter out on the streets! Damn!" said Jo. "And your dumb ass family is running around Miser blaming me, when you are the sole reason why Isabella is the way that she is. You've always enabled her to be dependent, and now that she is pregnant, you put her out. That's very smart of you CJ," said Jo sarcastically.

"Yeah, Jo. Yeah Yeah. I know everything my fault," said CJ, whining just like a little school kid.

"No! It's my fault," Jo said. "I made a huge ass mistake having kids with the likes of you. I should've known better than to believe you were actually going to look out for Isabella's best interest while she's pregnant."

CJ was speechless, and he knew not to say a word to Jo when she got angry.

"Look, I am on my way to Mississippi right now. If it's not asking too much of you, could you at least try to find out something about Isabella's where-a-bouts?" asked Jo. "You might want to start with that no good ass sister of yours, because she's the one who seems to think she knows everything."

Seven

The Mystery

When Jo arrived in Miser, she stopped at the gas station to gas up her car and saw Isabella's close friend Paula working there.

"Hello Paula," greeted Jo. "How have you been doing?"

"I've been doing ok Ms. Jo," answered Paula. "Working hard so I can give my kids the things I didn't have when I was growing up."

"How many kids do you have?" Jo asked.

"I have two kids now. A daughter and a son," answered Paula. "I'll be leaving here soon so I can pick them up from daycare."

"Paula, I'm not sure if you and Isabella are still friends, but," said Jo before Paula cut her off.

"Ms. Jo. Bella and I will always be friends. She's been living with me since her dad put her out," said Paula.

"How is she doing?" asked Jo.

"She's not doing too well. You know how Bella is. One minute she claims she is going to clean herself up, but the next minute she's high," said Paula. "I've been trying to help her as much as I can. Taking her to the doctor for checkups, but she's even making that hard."

"How?" asked Jo.

"The last time I took her to the doctor, she was so high, that she couldn't hide it. The doctor threatened to press charges against her, and arrange for the baby to go into state's custody at birth if she didn't clean herself up," said Paula concerned.

"How has she been since then?" asked Jo.

"Like I said Ms. Jo. One minute Bella says she's going to stop doing drugs, but the next minute she's high," said Paula. "After her last visit to the doctor, I reached out and asked Mr. CJ for help, but he acted like he didn't even care."

"Why do you say that?" asked Jo.

"He said, 'Shit on Bella. Let ha ass go. You can't help ha. Nobody can,'" said Paula, speaking like CJ in a low pitched voice.

"Do you know why CJ put Isabella out?" asked Jo.

"I'm not exactly sure what happened, because Bella rambles a lot when she's high," said Paula. "One night she was going on and on about being out in the streets, and how I was the only person who put up with her. I told her that she's lucky to have parents like you and Mr. CJ, and when I said that to her, she got so mad, pointed her fingers at me and said I didn't know what I was talking about. She told me I didn't know anything about you or her dad," said Paula.

"I really don't know what to do to help Isabella," said Jo. "If being pregnant doesn't make her want to do better with herself, I'm not sure what will. She's too old to be rebelling."

"Bella seemed to be ok at the beginning of her pregnancy. I'd see her about once a week, and she was going to work at the tree farm pretty regularly," Paula told Jo. "She started doing drugs again after her dad put her out. One night I asked her to tell me what was so bad in her life that was causing her to turn to drugs. She said, 'If you saw your daddy the way I saw mine, you'd do drugs too.' Because she speaks with so little details, I still don't know what she was talking about."

Jo hugged Paula as she said, "It's nice seeing you Paula, and thank you for everything. If it's ok with you, I'd like to go to your house to see if Isabella is there."

"Of course Ms. Jo. Anytime," said Paula.

"Take care of your children, and I'll be keeping in touch," said Jo as she waved and drove away from the gas station's pump area.

Eight

Straight Talk

Like every mother's first born child, Isabella held a special place in Jo's heart. As much a disappointment as Isabella was, Jo didn't lose one ounce of love for her, and if there was something Jo could do to save Isabella from her very on self-destruction, she would.

When Jo arrived at Paula's house, she saw Isabella sitting on the front porch.

"Hello Honey," greeted Jo, as she stepped out of the car and walked towards the front porch.

"Hey Ma," said Isabella. "What you doing here?"

"What! You're not happy to see me?" asked Jo, smiling.

"Yeah Ma, but I know you wouldn't be here in Miser unless something was wrong or you had business to attend to," said Isabella.

"Well you're right. I'm here checking on you," said Jo.

"Why you checking on me?" asked Isabella. "I'm alright."

"Get up, go look at yourself in the mirror, and then tell me you're okay," Jo said.

"If you came all the way here to preach to me, you can go back to Florida. Go back where you don't have to see me or my daddy. That's what you want anyway, right!" said Isabella, trying to start an argument.

"Look girl! I didn't drive all the way here to argue with you. I will get my happy ass back in the car and leave before I stand here and argue with you. I came here to say something to you, and I am going to say what I came here to say while you sit your pregnant ass there and listen," said Jo in an authoritative tone.

"Isabella, have you looked at yourself in the mirror lately? LOOK AT YOU! About to deliver a baby any minute, and you can barely keep your head up and your eyes open," Jo chastised. "What is wrong with you girl?"

"Stop calling me girl," said Isabella.

"Then grow up, and stop acting like a girl," said Jo. "What is it going to take for you to wake your ass up? What kind of mother are you planning to be to that child you're carrying?" asked Jo.

"See Ma, you trippin," said Isabella. "I don't want to hear all that shit. You came all the way here to judge me!"

"I raised you better than this Child," said Jo. "If you don't care about yourself, at least care about the baby you're about to deliver.

That's an innocent child who didn't even ask to come into this world," snapped Jo.

"I know!" said Isabella. "I don't know what to do. This baby about to come and I don't have nothing for him, or nowhere to go. It's cramped here at Paula's. I gotta share a room with her little girl, and I can't stand her boyfriend."

"When you are living with someone else, you don't get a say so or have choices, Isabella. Be grateful that Paula took you in when your daddy put you out," educated Jo.

"What did you do to make your daddy put you out? You should think about apologizing to him so you can have a home for your child," said Jo.

"I don't ever want to be around that man again. I have no respect for him, and I can't live with someone I have no respect for," said Isabella.

"What happened?" Jo asked.

"You don't want to know Ma," said Isabella.

"If it isn't my business, then no, I don't want to know. I just see that you are his and my daughter, who's pregnant, homeless, and refuse to stay with him for some unknown reason, so it is my business," said Jo.

Nine

All Fours

"Mom, I have been so angry with you for leaving my daddy and breaking our family up," said Isabella.

"Yeah Isabella, I've figured that much out, but I thought you wanted to see me happy," said Jo.

"Yeah, I want to see you happy, but you fooled around with that crazy dude who tried to kill you," said Isabella.

"So you are saying it is my fault that Psycho tried to kill me," Jo said.

"Yeah! You should've known not to deal with somebody crazy like that," said Isabella.

"You're right! I DID know better. That's why I ended the relationship with him. Girl you are so damn confused, I don't know where you come from half the time," said Jo.

"Isabella child, you must've been high when I went through that terrible ordeal with Psycho, or either you've had a memory lapse," said Jo. "Let me see if I can get my own story right. Once I figured out that Psycho was truly dangerous, I ended the relationship with him. He didn't want me to end our relationship, so he got angry with me for not wanting to be with him. He was so angry, that he broke into my house and tried to kill me. Not once, but twice."

"You don't have to retell the story," said Isabella angrily.

"Oh yes it seems I do," said Jo. "Now please tell me which part of almost losing my life by the hands of that Psycho individual is my fault. If you want to blame me go right ahead Isabella, because the way you are, I don't expect any different," said Jo.

"I know my daddy got his issues, but he never tried to kill you," said Isabella.

"Because by the time you came into this world, your dad had already killed me," said Jo.

"What are you talking about now?" asked Isabella.

"You won't understand, so I refuse to explain," said Jo. "Tell me what happened with you and your dad."

"I know you don't want to hear what I'm about to tell you Ma, but you asked so I'm gonna be honest with you," said Isabella, talking in circles.

"Spit it out Girl," Jo said.

"You remember Nick?" asked Isabella.

"Are you talking about that boy who was sweet on you?" ask Jo.

"Yeah him. He's the biggest drug dealer in Miser these days, and whenever I want a fix, I go to him," said Isabella.

"Please child. I really don't want to know the ins and outs of your drug habit," Jo said

"That's not why I told you that Ma," said Isabella. "Do you remember that tall man who was always across the tracks by MeMaw," she asked. "The one who dated daddy's sister Pam."

"Yes, I know who you're talking about," said Jo. "He used to hang back there by your daddy's mom's house all the time. With your Uncle Dale. You're right. He sure did date Pam for a while. I think his name is Jeremy."

"Yeah that's him!" confirmed Isabella. "Jeremy."

"Jeremy was a nice but strange man," said Jo. "A good carpenter too. I remember him coming to our house pretty often back then.

Most times he wanted your dad to take him someplace. Why are you telling me about him?" asked Jo.

"Mom, why you say Jeremy was strange?" asked Isabella.

"Well, even though he was much older than your dad, he appeared weak. Did whatever your dad and Dale told him to do. He was around a good bit, but never really had much to say to me," said Jo.

"I BET he DIDN'T have much to say to you Mom," said Isabella, with a for sure attitude.

"Why not?" asked Jo. "I was always nice to him."

"Cuz he was fucking Dad. Your husband," said Isabella. "That's why he didn't have much to say to you."

"What?" asked Jo.

"Ma, Jeremy is a crack head," said Isabella.

"I figured that out a long time ago. Most men and women who hung out by your memaw's house across the tracks were," said Jo. "People called them strawberries and blueberries. Please tell me you're not a strawberry Isabella."

"NO MA!" yelled Isabella. "I get drugs from my friend Nick. He still likes me so he gives me whatever I want."

"And what do you give him in return?" asked Jo.

"Nothing! You missing the whole point," said Isabella.

"Well get to the point," commanded Jo.

"I just told you Jeremy and Dad fuck each other," said Isabella looking at Jo with a matter of fact attitude. "Why are you ignoring what I just told you?"

"I heard you. How did you find out?" asked Jo.

"I found out the night I went to the Swamp Shack to meet Nick. Ms. Juanita, the old bartender who runs the Swamp Shack knew I was there looking for Nick, so she told me Nick was out back," said Isabella, telling her story. "I went out the front door and walked around the side of the building. When I got to side of the building, I saw a man bending down on all fours like a dog, and another man was fucking him from behind."

"That's why you shouldn't be at places like that," Jo fussed.

"Whatever Ma," said Isabella, impatiently. "I was there to get drugs from Nick, so I didn't care about them men or what they were doing."

"You need to stay your ass away from Nick and places like that," said Jo.

"I don't care about seeing two men having sex, because I see that all the time in the streets. At least I didn't care until I saw that the man bending on all fours like a dog was my own daddy," said Isabella. "With that old man Jeremy fucking him in his ass."

"I'm sorry you had to see that Honey," said Jo.

"Why don't you seem surprised?" Isabella asked full of anger.

"Because I'm not surprised," said Jo. "I'm just sorry you had to see that."

"You mean to tell me you already knew Dad was like that?" asked Isabella, still angry.

"I've suspected it for years," said Jo.

"How Mom? How did you figure it out?" asked Isabella.

"I put the puzzle pieces together. A bit too late, but I did," said Jo.

During Jo's marriage to CJ, she sensed his attraction to men. He sometimes said things to her that sent her mind off wondering. Jo always wondered why he preferred to spend time with certain guys instead of her.

The signs were there from the moment Jo met CJ, but her life was such a fog, she didn't notice. It was only after Jo took a step back from CJ and his family when the pieces started to come together.

CJ always made a point to be extra flirtatious with other women; especially in front of Jo. He went on annual man trips with a few of his cousins and close friends. When the men were on their trips in Miami, Dallas, or Vegas, they frequented strip clubs. During their strip club visits, CJ's cousins and friends would stay in the general public area of the club where the women were stripping on stage, but CJ always went in the back, to one of the private rooms. CJ would disappear for hours. CJ was so insecure and didn't want anyone to suspect his homosexuality that he always made a point to go out of his way to interact with women when others were around to observe. That was a way of masking his true identity, or sexual preference.

CJ did not dress like a real man until Jo taught him how to. She insisted that he dress like a decent gentleman when they went out in public together. If it was up to CJ, he'd wear every color of the rainbow at the same time.

Besides going out of his way to mask his homosexuality and try to prove his manhood, he had a huge drinking problem.

"Isabella, when most people drink to the point of alcoholism like your dad, it's usually because they are trying to suppress something," said Jo.

Ten

Small World

A few days later, Isabella gave birth to a little baby boy, and she named him Preston. Jo never dreamed of becoming a grandmother, but there she was, blessed with the most beautiful grandson ever. From the very first moment Jo laid her eyes on Preston, her heart belonged to him.

Since Isabella was a drug user during her pregnancy, Preston was born with Neonatal Abstinence Syndrome and needed to stay in the hospital longer than usual. As much as Jo missed her home in Florida and couldn't wait to get back, she stayed in Miser as long as Preston was in the hospital. Jo went to the hospital each day and sat with Preston. As she watched his tiny little body suffer, she grew angry with Isabella. In addition to being mad with Isabella, Jo blamed herself.

One evening when Jo was walking out of the hospital, she heard someone call her name from behind.

"Jo," someone called.

Jo turned around to see who was calling her.

"Jo, is that you?" asked the gentleman.

Squinting her eyes to see who was approaching her from a distance Jo said with question, "Lonny?"

"Jo! Lonny!" said Jo and Lonny in unison, as they hugged one another. "What are you doing here?" they said right before laughing, because they kept speaking in unison.

"I work here at Miser Memorial," said Lonny, "as one of the on-call anesthesiologist."

"Are you living in Miser these days?" asked Jo.

"Yes, I'm living here now. How are you and your husband doing?" Lonny asked.

"Lonny, I have been divorced for several years now," said Jo.

"Are you in a rush to go someplace? Do you have time to talk? Have you had dinner?" Lonny anxiously asked.

"I can eat," said Jo with a smile.

Jo and Lonny met at Waffle House, which was one of Jo's favorite places to eat. The two sat in the Waffle House for three hours catching up on each other's lives.

Just like Jo, Lonny had married and divorced. He fathered two daughters around the same age as Jo's girls, with his wife, who cheated on him while their youngest daughter was still an infant. Lonny continued to live in

56

New Orleans after his divorce, and he had custody of his daughters, because his ex-wife was unable to provide a safe and stable home for their girls.

Lonny told Jo that he had recently moved from New Orleans to Miser to be mental support for his youngest daughter Ann, who was taking care of her sick mother. His ex-wife.

"Ann is pregnant right now. She's been a handful her whole life and Candy made it pretty easy for her to be promiscuous," said Lonny.

Jo listened attentively to every single word Lonny said, and when she needed to ask a question to keep up, she did.

"Your younger daughter's name is Ann?" asked Jo, "and your ex-wife's name is Candy?"

"Yes," answered Lonny.

"Where is Candy now?" asked Jo.

"Candy lives here in Miser. She's been very sick lately. In and out of the hospital," answered Lonny.

"Miser Memorial?" asked Jo.

"Oh No. She goes to the charity hospital in D'Iberville, Mississippi," said Lonny.

"I'm sorry to hear that your ex-wife is sick," said Jo.

"No need to apologize to me Jo. She planted her seeds and she is right where she should be. She made that bed for herself. I just feel bad that her three daughters, two which are mine, are losing their mother," said Lonny.

"Oh, she's dying?" asked Jo.

"Yes. She has an acquired immune deficiency syndrome," said Lonny.

"Is that," asked Jo.

"Yes," Lonny quickly replied as he cut Jo off.

"Does Candy have a man in her life right now?" asked Jo.

"Yes, some dude name Calvin. Ann calls him CJ," Lonny said. "But from what I hear, he has issues of his own. Ann says he's always drunk, and Candy is sick of him."

"There aren't many women with the name Candy, who has three daughters, with the youngest named Ann," thought Jo, as Lonny continued to talk. Once Lonny got to a stopping point, Jo shared her new found discovery.

"Lonny, it's a small world," said Jo.

"Yes it is, but what makes you say that right now?" asked Lonny.

"I know Candy, Ann, and CJ very well," said Jo.

"You do? How?" asked Lonny.

"I know CJ and Candy as two pieces of trash who met on the bottom of a dumpster," said Jo, as she continued to tell Lonny about Candy being her neighbor, their daughters becoming friends, the mother daughter summer trip to California, and how Candy and CJ ended up together.

Lonny was speechless after hearing Jo's summary of how his ex-wife Candy and her ex-husband CJ ended up together.

Eleven

No Clue

When Jo's grandson was released from the hospital, she took him and Isabella with her to Florida. Jo arranged to get Preston's medical records transferred to a pediatrician in Florida, and she laid out her house rules and expectations to Isabella. Determined to help Isabella become a good mother for Preston, Jo preached to and coached Isabella every chance she got.

"Isabella, you are Preston's mother, and you will take care of him," said Jo. "I expect you to stay off of drugs and get a job so you can pay your share of the living expenses around here. In addition to that, I'd like you to get your stuff together so you'll be ready to go to college when the new semester starts," said Jo.

"I promise I'll do better. I know I gotta stay off drugs. I ain't stupid. I have a child now, so I have to do right," Isabella said, trying to assure her mother she'd be much better than she had been before.

"If you want a better life, you have to make better choices. You have a child now, and it's your responsibility to take care of him. You can start by making yourself presentable so you can get a job worth having. Stop smoking, because the stale smoke in your clothes and hair smells horrible. Grow up and be a mother that Preston won't be embarrassed to call Mom," said Jo.

Isabella listened to her mother, and she seemed to be grateful that Jo took her and Preston in. On the other hand, Jo didn't take anything Isabella told her to heart, because Isabella was just like her dad CJ; full of empty promises. She had no clue, no respect, and no work ethic.

Not too long after Isabella got settled in and learned her way around Florida, she got a job working as a hostess in one of the local restaurants. For a new mother, she did a pretty good job taking care of Preston, with Jo's assistance of course. When the spring semester came around, Isabella enrolled in college at Florida State University, just as her mother asked her to do. Her life was pretty busy, and she did not have time to find trouble if she wanted to. Sometimes Isabella started to feel sorry for herself and complain about every little thing.

"It ain't fair," Isabella said to Jo. "Preston's dad don't do nothing. I gotta do everything."

"Welcome to motherhood," said Jo. "You're walking around here crying and complaining about how hard you have it. Feeling sorry for yourself! Girl, you don't know what hard is. You better wake up and count your blessings," Jo fussed.

"Well I'm here raising this child all by myself. Her daddy ain't shit. He's no help. If I didn't have you, I don't know what I would do," Isabella said.

"Stop looking at what you don't have and be grateful for what you do have," said Jo. "Please tell me where someone your age with a baby can go and live for just two hundred fifty dollars a month? When you flick a switch, the lights come on. When you go to wash your ass, the water comes out of the faucet. You have a full and clean functioning laundry room to use, air and heat, and an in home babysitter at your beck and call. What the hell are you sitting your ass here complaining about?"

After Jo's rant, Isabella settled down and started to think about the things Jo said to her.

Most days, Isabella woke up early and went to school. While she was at school, Jo took care of Preston. She'd prepare and feed him breakfast, give him a morning bath, dress him, pack a diaper bag, and bring him to daycare. When Isabella finished school for the day, she picked Preston up from daycare and spent time with him at home until Jo got off of work. After Jo arrived home from work each evening, Isabella left to go to work at the restaurant. Jo was home taking care of Preston every evening, after a long day of work. Jo had a manageable routine until Isabella started taking advantage of her.

"Mom, is it ok for me to hang out with my friends a little while after work?" Isabella asked.

Since Isabella had been working a lot of hours and keeping up in her college classes, Jo didn't see any harm in allowing Isabella to hang out a few hours after work with her friends every once in a while.

"That is fine Isabella," said Jo. "Just please be sure to come and get the baby monitor from my room when you get in."

When Jo was responsible for Preston, she didn't rest or sleep much, because she gave him her undivided attention. Jo loved Preston more than anything in the world, and she cherished every moment with him. Most evenings, Jo and Preston had dinner time first, and then bath time.

Preston was approaching one, and he developed such an attractive and playful personality. Like any child that age, he kept Jo on her feet, and there was never a still dull moment. Even after Preston went to sleep, Jo still didn't rest well, because she listened out for him. Anytime Preston moved or made a sound,

Jo checked on him. She was up through the night checking to make sure he was alright.

As time continued to go by and Preston continued to grow more active, Isabella took that much more advantage of Jo's love for Preston. There were nights Isabella stayed out late, and when she finally got in, she didn't announce her return or relieve Jo of baby monitor duty. When morning came, Jo still had her usual routine of getting herself and Preston together for the day. In addition, she still had to go to work, no matter how tired she was from lack of sleep.

Jo worked close to forty hours a week at UPS and she put in as much time as she could supervising design jobs at the condominium. In addition to all those work hours, she continued to be active in Preston's life, and Isabella continued to take her for granted.

Twelve

Exhaustion

Over time, Jo felt her body growing weak, but she didn't think much of it. As busy as she'd been working and going nonstop at home with Preston, it was no wonder why she'd been feeling more tired than usual. Jo knew she wasn't getting the proper amount of sleep, but she didn't fret about it because she loved every moment she spent with her grandson. Preston was Jo's joy, and she was always so wrapped up in giving Preston her undivided attention, that she chose to ignore all warning signs of exhaustion until the day came when her body would not allow her to ignore it any longer.

One evening Jo was sitting at the desk in her working office located at the new condominiums. She was sketching out a floor plan for furniture placement in the two bedroom condos, when a sudden pain arose in her chest. Immediately following that sharp pain, nausea grew on her like never before, and saliva started to build up in Jo's mouth. As weak as Jo was feeling from the pain and nausea, she mustered up just enough energy to reach for the small garbage can located underneath her desk. Just as she pulled the garbage can from underneath her desk, she started throwing up large amounts of liquid. Jo had no energy to get up or move, so she sat there bent over with her head down on the desk.

Jo was extremely weak with little to no energy, and she felt like she was dying. With her head on her desk, she opened her eyes just enough to see her cell phone sitting on her desk to the far right. Slowly but surely, Jo slid her right hand towards the cell phone. Once her hand was right next to the phone, she rested it on top, and slid it towards her, because she didn't have enough energy to pick it up. With one finger, Jo touched the phone's screen to get to her contacts, and pressed for the phone to call Kamryn, a designer who worked for her.

"Hello," said Kamryn.

Jo had no energy to lift her head or hold the phone up to her ear, so she talked towards the phone while it sat there on the desk.

"Kamryn, I feel very sick," said Jo.

"Where are you?" asked Kamryn.

"In my office at the condos," Jo answered weakly.

"I'm on my way," said Kamryn with a sense of urgency.

Kamryn arrived at Jo's office about fifteen minutes later, and when she took one look at Jo, she called 911 without hesitation. Soon after she made that call, the emergency medical technicians arrived and began working on Jo immediately.   While they were pulling out equipment, and attaching different things to her, they asked Kamryn a few basic questions.

"How old is she? Does she have any allergies that you know of? Has she been sick lately? Can you tell us what happened?"

Kamryn wasn't able to answer many of those questions, because Jo was such a private person who never shared personal things about herself with others.

On the commute to the hospital, Jo lost consciousness, and later that night she awoke in the hospital wondering where she was and how she'd gotten there.

"Kamryn, will you please find my phone and call Isabella to let her know what's going on," said Jo.

Kamryn located Jo's phone and made that call right then, in front of Jo.

"Hello Isabella. This is Ms. Kamryn. I'm calling to let you know that I am here with your mom at the hospital. She isn't doing very well," said Kamryn.

"What am I going to do?" Isabella asked selfishly. "If mom is in the hospital, who's gonna watch Preston?"

Silence fell over the phone, because Kamryn didn't know how to reply to the things Isabella had said.

"How long they gonna keep her in there?" asked Isabella.

"I am not sure how long they are going to keep her in here, but when I find out more, I'll let you know," said Kamryn.

"Damn! Alright," Isabella said rudely, before she hung up the phone.

Jo spent several nights and days in the hospital, and after doctors ran a series of tests, she was diagnosed with Diastolic Heart Failure and Multiple Sclerosis. When Jo was finally discharged from the hospital, she went home with countless bottles of medication.

At home, feeling weaker than ever, Jo began to worry. Even though she was very sick and limited to what she could do, Isabella still left Preston alone with her. Isabella had no consideration or one ounce of concern for her mother or Preston's wellbeing. The only thing Isabella cared about was hanging out with her friends and getting high every chance she got.

"What is going to happen to Preston if something happens to me?" worried Jo. "I need to get my affairs in order."

With those thoughts beating up her mind, Jo called her best friend Carmen, who was still living in Mississippi. Jo wanted to make sure Carmen still knew what to do if something happened to her. After speaking to Carmen, Jo called her younger daughter

Jaylynn. She hated to call Jaylynn, better known as the biggest worry wart, but she felt it was only right. Jaylynn needed to know what was going on with her.

"Is Bella helping you out?" Jaylynn asked.

"You know your sister. She's not even here," answered Jo.

"Where did they go?" asked Jaylynn.

"Preston is here with me. Just your sister is gone," said Jo.

"What! Correct me if I'm wrong. You did just get out of the hospital, right?" asked Jaylynn.

"Yes," Jo answered weakly.

"Why are you allowing Bella to leave Preston with you?" Jaylynn asked angrily.

"You know how your sister is Jaylynn. I don't have enough energy to argue or fight with her. Plus Preston is better off with me, even if I am sick," said Jo.

"It seems like you're barely able to take care of yourself. Heart failure can't be good, and you sound weak," said Jaylynn. "Doesn't that make you weak?" she asked. "And exactly what is Multiple Sclerosis?"

"It's nothing too serious honey. Nothing you need to worry about. I'll be just fine after I build my energy back up," said Jo.

Thirteen

Sibling Duel

Jaylynn knew that her mother always held back information, so she called Carmen as soon as she got off of the phone with Jo. She wanted to make sure her mother told her everything and didn't hold back any important or need to know information. After speaking to Carmen, it was just as she'd thought.

"Jaylynn, your mother is a very sick woman," said Carmen.

"If she is that sick, why is she telling me she's just fine and all she needs to do is build up her energy?" asked Jaylynn.

"You know how your mother is. She's always watering down problems. And your sister isn't any help over there. If you ask me, I think she is a huge contributor towards your mother being sick," said Carmen.

"I think you're right Ms. Carmen," said Jaylynn.

Jaylynn learned that her mother was indeed a very sick woman, and Isabella was still up to no good like always. The more she thought about everything, the madder she became.

"Bella lives in the same house as Mom," said Jaylynn to Carmen during their phone conversation. "I'd think my own sister would call and tell me something about our mother going into the hospital."

Jaylynn's anger grew and grew to a point where she was walking around her dorm room cursing the air out as if it was Isabella. In order to get her sanity back, and to clear the air, she thought it would be best to call Isabella.

"Hey Bella. Where are you?" asked Jaylynn, when Isabella answered the phone.

"None of your business. Why? What's your problem?" Isabella asked.

"Why didn't you call and tell me Mom was in the hospital?" asked Jaylynn calmly.

"I don't have to call and tell your spoiled ass shit," said Isabella. "Go back to your little fancy dorm room with your fancy friends and polish your toenails."

Jaylynn did not want to argue with Isabella, so she refused to make a comment on her ugly remarks. Instead, she chose to stick to the reason she called.

"Are you helping mom around there, or are you still leaving your child for her to take care of while you run the streets chasing after drugs?" Jaylynn asked, striking back in her own way.

"Fuck you! Worry about your damn self and stop worrying about what I'm doing, Little Girl," said Isabella.

"I see you haven't changed and probably never will. You're still selfish and don't care about anyone else. You're probably the reason why Mom is sick. Always causing problems and needing her to clean up your mess," Jaylynn said angrily. "I can't stand you. You don't have enough sense to know you're frying the little brain cells you have. Just like dad and his family. Stupid as ever and not worth the air you breathe," she concluded, right before hanging up the phone.

There was no way Jaylynn was going to sit back and allow Isabella's drama and lack of consideration to run their mother to an early grave. After that phone conversation, Jaylynn immediately jumped into a problem solving mode just like her mother normally would do when she was feeling well. She looked at the school calendar to see when the semester would end, and decided it was best to do whatever she had to do in order to transfer to a college in Florida, closer to her mother.

Fourteen

Life Saver

Since it was the end of the spring
semester and summer was beginning, Jaylynn
packed her personal belongings in her car, and
drove from Colorado to Florida. She moved in
with her mother, and helped out every way she
could. Even though Jo said and did everything
she could to convince Jaylynn to stay in
Colorado and live her own life, she felt blessed
to have Jaylynn there with her. With Jaylynn's
help, Jo didn't feel as pressed or drained.

Even though Jaylynn despised her older
sister Isabella, she fell in instant love with her

nephew Preston. Preston became the light in Jaylynn's eyes, and she became his biggest protector.

The house was most peaceful when Isabella wasn't around, but when she was home, the dark cloud that hovered over her was in the house too. Isabella was very negative, never satisfied, never had anything nice to say to or about anyone, and was extremely ungrateful. When she was home, she started arguments with Jaylynn quite often, and Jo spent a lot of time being a buffer between the two girls.

"Stop all that arguing. Preston does not need to see you two acting this way," Jo would say.

"Mom, you need to put Bella out. She's no good around here anyway. Not before I came here and sure not now," said Jaylynn.

"Fuck you Jaylynn. Who are you to tell her to put me out? This ain't your house and I belong here just as much as you do," Isabella yelled.

To discontinue the loud arguing, Jaylynn walked out into the backyard, and right after, Isabella slammed the front door as she stormed out. After Jo checked on Preston, she went into the backyard to talk to Jaylynn.

"Jay, you know how your sister is. She'll do anything to start a fight. You can't entertain her foolishness and whatever you do, don't let anything she says get to you," said Jo.

"Mom, she's no help around here, so I don't know why you allow her to live here and disrespect you in your own house," said Jaylynn.

"I do what I do and put up with certain things for Preston's sake. She is his mother," Jo said. "I don't want to begin to imagine what kind of life he'd have if he wasn't here with me. And I'm so glad you are in his life now."

"I love him so much, Mom. He's so cute, and lovable. Just like you say he's your joy, he's my joy too," said Jaylynn.

As the days, weeks, and months went by, Jo realized the medicine the doctors put her on wasn't helping her any. Her energy level was lower than it had ever been before, and she was convinced it was the medication causing that. Without discussing it with her doctor, Jo took herself off of all the medication, and shortly after, her strength built back up and she was able to resume the routine she had before.

Since Jaylynn was around to help care for and entertain Preston, Jo went back to work a few hours a week in the office at UPS, and in time, she finished the design job at one condominium and started another one. Her daily life was pretty much back to normal, and she didn't seem to have as much worry or fear weighing on her. With the girls and Preston around, Jo's mind didn't wonder back to her bad past as much as it did before.

Fifteen

Concealment

Jo was home with Preston, and the house was quiet and peaceful as it always was when Isabella wasn't there. Jo took care of Preston like she always did. She prepared a light dinner for three, fed Preston, ate dinner herself, put dinner on the side for the girls, cleaned the kitchen, gave Preston a bath, put him in his pajamas, and prepared for their evening story time. After story time, Preston went down for the night, and only then was when Jo was finally able to relax.

When Jaylynn came in from school and work, she usually ate first, took a shower, and settled down to study.

"Give me the baby monitor, Mom," said Jaylynn. "I'll listen out for Preston until Isabella comes in. You need to get some rest so you don't get sick."

"I don't know what I'd do without you," said Jo, as she gave Jaylynn a hug and goodnight kiss on the cheek.

Jo slept very well that night, and before she knew it, she was waking up to the sound of her alarm. Like always, she got up out of bed, went into the kitchen, and fixed herself a large glass of water. After gulping it down, she went back into her bedroom to get ready for work. Just as she was stepping out of the shower, she heard a knock on the bathroom door.

"Mom," said Jaylynn quietly.

"Is everything alright?" asked Jo.

"Isabella never came home last night," said Jaylynn.

"Did you try to call her?" asked Jo.

"Yes, but her phone goes straight to voicemail. Mom, Isabella is probably in some kind of trouble. You know how she is," said Jaylynn.

"Your sister hasn't been in any trouble since she's been living here with me." Jo said.

"I don't trust her Mom," said Jaylynn. "And I don't know how you can stand here and defend her."

"I'm not defending your sister. Just giving her the benefit of the doubt," said Jo. "I know she is selfish and very hard to take, but everyone needs a second chance at some point in life."

"From what I know, she's used up her second chance years ago," said Jaylynn.

"Don't worry about your sister. Everything will be alright," said Jo, trying to convince herself at the same time not to worry.

"I'm not worried about Isabella," said Jaylynn. "I don't care what happens to her. She can die tomorrow for all I care. I'm just worried about Preston. He got a sorry ass momma."

Jo didn't like to hear Jaylynn talk like that, but there wasn't much she could say in response, because Jaylynn was speaking the truth.

Days went by with no word from Isabella. Jo and Jaylynn called the county jail to see if she was in there, and they also called every hospital in the area, with no luck. In search of Isabella, the two exhausted all options, short of filing a missing persons report.

Jo and Jaylynn didn't know what else to do, so they continued their daily routines. Jaylynn went to school on the days she had school and work on the days she had work. The two women worked around each other's schedules in order to be there for Preston.

Long hours working at the design firm in addition to extra hours caring for Preston started to take a toll on Jo. Her health started to decline once again, and symptoms began to set in permanently. Her legs hurt on most days, and she was experiencing muscle spasms more often than before. Jo's arms were very weak, she was often attacked by dizziness, and sometimes the tremor in her hands were so bad, she couldn't perform the simplest of duties. Jo tried to hide her symptoms from everyone, but she couldn't hide them from Kamryn.

"You haven't been feeling well lately have you?" Kamryn asked.

"I'm alright," answered Jo, trying to shrug off Kamryn's question.

"Jo, I know you haven't been feeling well for some time now, and you've been doing everything you can to mask your pain," said Kamryn.

"How do you know?" asked Jo.

"I've been working with you long enough to know you. For a sick woman, you've taken on too many responsibilities. You go to work at UPS, and then you spend hours managing all aspects of every design job you have," answered Kamryn.

"That's what I choose to do Kamryn, because I enjoy my work," said Jo.

"I don't know exactly what's going on with your health, but I am cognizant enough to know you aren't well," said Kamryn. "Why don't you let me help you out more?" she asked. "I have nothing but time on my hands."

Jo did not want to admit the things Kamryn was telling her, but her body wouldn't allow her to do otherwise. She knew the time was coming for her to slow down and make some changes in her daily life, but she didn't want to quit her job at UPS. The health insurance she had through them was a great big help, and she didn't want to lose that.

After careful consideration, Jo decided to take a leave of absence, and she filled out necessary paperwork in order to keep the health insurance. In addition to that, Jo put Kamryn in charge of all projects at the design firm, and sat down with Jaylynn to have a serious talk.

Jo informed Jaylynn of all the changes she was making, and she quickly summarized the way she wanted her business affairs to be handled when she could no longer handle them herself.

"When something happens to me, be sure to contact Carmen immediately. She knows where all necessary paperwork is, exactly what to do, and who to contact," Jo said to Jaylynn.

"Why are you telling me all of this? Did the doctor tell you something you're not telling me?" asked Jaylynn. "You're not going to die anytime soon are you?"

"We all will die one day Jaylynn, and when I do, I want you to be prepared," said Jo.

"When did you go to the doctor? What did he tell you? He must've told you something for you to be talking this crazy nonsense," Jaylynn badgered.

"Any word on your sister?" Jo asked, avoiding Jaylynn's questions.

"No. I don't know why you worry about her anyway. She don't care about you! It's best to just forget about her," said Jaylynn angrily.

"Jaylynn, no matter how messed up your sister is, she's still my daughter and I'll always love her. If you ever become a mother, maybe you'll understand," said Jo.

Sixteen

Fault

Many months went by, and Jo's health continued to decline rapidly. Jaylynn wanted to spend every waking moment with her mother, but Jo refused to allow her daughter to give up her young free life.

"Jaylynn, my illness prevents me from doing things that I'd like to do, but I will not sit here and allow my sickness to prevent you from living and growing the way I had a chance to do when I was your age," said Jo. "Your presence alone is a huge blessing, and I am very grateful that you are here with Preston and me, but I don't want you to stop living your life the best that you can," said Jo.

"But I'm here to help you, Mom," said Jaylynn.

"And that is exactly what you are doing each and every day. In your sister's absence, you've stepped up and taken care of Preston better than she ever had. That alone is a huge responsibility Jaylynn, so I don't want you worrying about me. I am going to be sick with or without you worrying, so enjoy your life as much as you can. Time isn't promised to any of us, so I want you to make the best of your time," said Jo.

"How can I make the best of it when I know you're here dying?" Jaylynn asked.

"I am still living, so in the meantime, I don't want you or anyone standing over me with tears, acting or treating me like I am already dead," said Jo. "Try having a little trust in God, and know he does things in his time," said Jo.

"You're always talking about God. How can you sit here and speak about trusting in God after all he's put you through?" asked Jaylynn.

"God didn't put me through anything," answered Jo. "Why are you so angry?" she asked.

"I'm NOT angry," barked Jaylynn.

"Then why are you getting upset?" Jo asked.

"Mom, I don't know what I am going to do after you are gone," said Jaylynn with tears in her eyes.

"You'll continue to live, so please stop ruining the present by thinking about the future," Jo said.

"How can you be so positive with everything that has happened?" asked Jaylynn.

"Things don't just happen to us, Child. The choices we make bring certain things into our lives. Before I married your dad, he showed me the type of person he was. Just like Maya

Angelou said, 'When someone shows you who they are, believe them the first time.' Your dad showed me who he was from the very beginning of our relationship, but I believed I could change him and married him anyway. I thought if I loved him enough, he'd start loving me just as much in return, and want to be a better person for me," said Jo.

"Yeah, but what about all that stuff you went through with Psycho?" asked Jaylynn

"That was my fault too. I chose to be with him, even though I knew he was an alcoholic and a dope head. I chose to trust the wrong person," answered Jo.

"Okay. What about Mawmaw and Pawpaw dying. Is that your fault too? I guess Candy and my dad being together is your fault too. The way Isabella is. Her addiction to drugs. Her missing in action and not even mothering her own child. All that is your fault too, right?" stated Jaylynn, with a smart ass attitude.

"Your grandparents passing was God's will. He will take all of us when he's good and ready, so no, that was not my doing. Candy and your dad being together is not my fault, because they are two grown people who choose to live without morals and respect. I won't take any blame for their evil doings. On the other hand, I do blame myself for your sister's shortcomings. As a mother, I should've known not to expose you and your sister to your dad's family. They were never good for themselves, and definitely no good for others; especially innocent children like you and Isabella once were," Jo said.

"Well Isabella is not an innocent child anymore. She has an innocent child of her own, and she should know better," said Jaylynn.

"You're right. She should know better, even though she acts like she doesn't. Your sister is weak minded. She's weak just like the

Sims. Don't have her priorities straight, and has no willpower. Isabella has always been a follower and admired all of the wrong people," said Jo.

"I have no respect for Isabella," said Jaylynn.

"I understand why you don't respect her, but you do love her, right?" asked Jo.

"She's my sister, so I guess I have to," replied Jaylnn.

Seventeen

Pain and Peace

A year later, Jo was still hanging on, and Carmen drove to Florida as often as she could to be there with her. Jo enjoyed Carmen's company, and she really appreciated the warm feeling of family and life that Carmen's presence brought into her home. The two longtime friends laughed their hearts out, as they reminisced about the good old days.

"Remember the year we took our very first road trip to Atlanta?" asked Carmen.

"How can I forget? We drove all the way from Miser to Atlanta with the top down on the convertible," said Jo.

"We were both sunburnt by the time we made it there, but that sure was fun," said Carmen laughing.

"Do you remember that year we celebrated your fiftieth birthday, and you insisted on wearing that crazy looking hat?" Jo asked as she laughed hard.

"Be quiet!" said Carmen. "Nothing was wrong with my hat."

Jo was laughing so hard, and she started to cough.

"Here, drink some water," said Carmen as she was handing Jo a glass.

Once Jo's coughing subsided, she dozed off and took a long nap. While Jo was napping, Jaylynn and Preston made it home, and the two sat and had dinner with Carmen. After dinner, Jaylen got Preston ready for bedtime, and

Carmen read him a bedtime story. When Carmen read to Preston, she got deep into character, Preston broke into laughter and said, "Do it again T Carmen, do it again!"

Preston was growing so fast, and he'd developed such a cute little personality.

Jaylynn was having a hard time knowing that her mother was dying, but she continued to stand strong like Jo asked her to do. Many days it was very hard for Jaylynn to hide her weakness, but she made a point not to show it in front of her mother. During harder times, Jaylynn retreated to her bedroom or went into the bathroom to soak in a tub of hot bubbly water and tears. On days when Jaylynn could not find comfort from within, she shared her feelings with Carmen in hopes of gaining a little comfort.

"I don't know what I am going to do when Mom is gone," Jaylynn said to Carmen.

"Jay, you'll do exactly as your Mom has asked you to do. Live your life. She wouldn't want it any other way," said Carmen.

Jaylynn started to cry. "I don't want to lose her," she said.

"I know you love your mother, and it is hard to lose people we love. Trust me when I tell you that you'll be alright. In time, this will be part of the past, and you'll be just fine," said Carmen.

"That's exactly what mom told me," said Jaylynn.

"Everyone handles death and emotions differently. Your Mom says, 'When people cut up and act out after losing a loved one, that's tears of guilt, but when they know they've done right by the person they've lost, their reaction isn't as extreme or dramatic.' From where I stand, you should not have one tear of guilt or regret where your mother is concerned. Your mother took the loss of her parents very hard,

but not once did many see her act out," said
Carmen.

"That's true. During that time I knew
she was dealing with a lot, and I still didn't see
her cry," said Jaylnn. "When I was younger,
Dad and I always told her she was heartless
when she didn't cry about something we
thought she should cry about."

"Your mother cried day after day when
she lost your grandparents. You know she is the
type of person who does not like people to know
her pain or her happiness. She says, 'When
people know your pain, they make it worse, and
when they know your happiness, they try to ruin
it,'" Carmen quoted Jo.

Later that night, Carmen woke with an
uneasy feeling in her stomach. Something told
her to go and check on Jo, so she walked slowly
and quietly down the hallway to Jo's bedroom,
and she saw her sitting up in the recliner next to
her bed.

"Jo, what are you doing up at this time of the night?" Carmen asked.

"I love to watch Preston sleep," said Jo.

"Yes, children are the cutest and most peaceful when they sleep," Carmen agreed, as she wondered why Jo was telling her that.

"I got up to walk to Preston's room, because I wanted to watch him sleep. When I stood up, my legs were too weak, so I sat here. Do you think you could help me walk in there?" asked Jo.

"Yes. I'll get the walker and bring it closer," said Carmen.

When Jo made it to Preston's bedroom, she sat on his bed, and rubbed his dirty blonde hair while he slept. She found so much comfort and peace when she watched him sleep, and after a while, she dozed off. The following morning Jaylynn went into Preston's bedroom to wake him up for the day, and she found her mother asleep next to him.

"Look at her," thought Jaylynn, as she watched her mother sleep. "She looks more peaceful than she has ever looked in a very long time."

When Jaylynn walked back into the kitchen, Carmen was in there making herself a cup of coffee.

"Did you help Mom get to Preston's room last night?" Jaylynn asked.

"Yes. She wanted to watch Preston sleep," Carmen answered.

Later that evening Jo and Carmen sat out on the deck facing the beach. Jo loved the sun, and she loved to feel it on her skin. The two friends enjoyed the peaceful silence, and even though words weren't spoken, their conversation was one of the deepest they'd ever had. After watching the sunset, and preparing to go back inside, Jo said, "I think it's time to take me to the hospital Carmen."

Eighteen

How Long?

"Your mom is ready to go to the hospital, so I will bring her shortly," Carmen told Jaylynn.

"Is it time for us to do those things Mom asked us to do?" Jaylen asked.

"Yes, I think it's time," answered Carmen.

Immediately after that conversation, Jaylynn called Kamryn to let her know Carmen was taking her mother to the hospital. As soon as Kamryn got that phone call from Jaylynn, she grabbed her car keys and drove to Jo's cottage

107

to stay with Preston while Jaylynn went to the hospital to be with her mother. When Kamryn arrived at the cottage, Jaylynn gave her a long hard hug and said, "Thank you!" right before she walked out of the door.

Shortly after Jaylynn arrived at the hospital, Dr. Leomoni came in.

"How's she doing?" asked Jaylynn.

"Come out into the waiting room so we can let your mother rest," Dr. Leomoni whispered.

The doctor lead the way and Jaylynn and Carmen followed behind him. Once they were all in the waiting room, the three sat down.

"How is she doing?" Jaylynn asked again with the sound of impatience and anxiety in her voice.

"Jaylynn, your mother is blessed to have hung on this long. She's not doing well at all, and now would be a good time to call any other family members to see her. Depending on her faith, you may want to call a clergyman," said Dr. Leomoni.

"How long do you think she has?" asked Jaylynn.

"Based on her illness and the stages of dying, she's in the last stages," answered the doctor. "It could be a day or two. Even more. I know your mother is a faithful woman, so I am going to tell you just like she told me. 'It's in God's hands, and it'll happen in His time.'"

As the doctor spoke, Carmen nodded her head agreeing and showing that she understood everything he was saying.

"If you need anything, please don't hesitate to call me. The nurses here will keep a good eye on Jo, and keep her as comfortable as possible," said Dr. Leomoni.

When the doctor left, Carmen stayed seated so she could talk to Jaylynn alone.

"Jay, I think you should make some phone calls to some relatives in Miser, and try to get in touch with your sister to tell her what's going on," said Carmen.

"Carmen, you know how my mother feels about Miser and the people in it," said Jaylynn. "So I am not going to call anyone. If they were an important part of Mom's life, they'd already know what's going on, and be here like we are."

"Isabella is your mother's daughter, and she deserves the right to know that her mother is dying," said Carmen.

"If you want to tell her, you tell her. That's if you can even find her," said Jaylynn.

Carmen left the hospital to make the one phone call Jo told her to make when this time in her life came.

"Hello," answered Jo's cousin Tamara.

"Hi. My name is Carmen, Jo's friend," said Carmen.

"Yes, I remember meeting you at my Uncle's funeral," said Tamara.

"I am here in Florida with Jo right now. I'm not sure if you or anyone else in the family knew of her illness. She's in the hospital right now, and she doesn't have much time left to live. If you know how to get in touch with Isabella, I think she needs to know," said Carmen.

"I'm sorry to hear about Jo. She and I were very close for years, until...Thank you for calling me Carmen. I'll definitely do my best to let Isabella know," Tamara said, with regret in her voice.

Nineteen

Mouth of the South

Years before when Jo found out she was very sick, she had a long talk with Carmen about her will, and how she wanted things to be handled.

"Jaylynn is extremely bitter towards her sister," Jo said to Carmen during their talk. "She does not like to communicate with Isabella, and in the event of me dying, I doubt she would even call her sister to tell her. In the event Jaylynn decides to put her feelings to the side and call her sister like I've asked her to do, there's no guarantee that she'll be able to get in touch with her," said Jo.

"If something happens, I'll call Isabella," said Carmen.

"No. I don't want you to call Isabella. She'll be hard to reach anyway, because she never has a phone," said Jo. "But there is one, just one phone call that I do want you to make when that time comes," said Jo.

"To who?" asked Carmen.

"My cousin Tamara. She's the mouth of the south. Mississippi Motor Mouth is what many call her. If you call her, word will travel fast, and the message will get to Isabella quicker than a bolt of lightening," said Jo.

Carmen made that one phone call like Jo asked her to do, and Jo was right. All it took was that one phone call to Tamara. The news about Jo dying traveled through Miser faster than the speed of light.

Within minutes, Carmen received a phone call from Isabella.

"Is it true what I hear about my momma?" Isabella asked, without even saying hello to Carmen.

"Hello Isabella. The doctor told us to notify family," said Carmen. .

"So she dying?" asked Isabella. "Where is Preston?"

"Your mother has been sick for a very long time now, and Jaylynn has been taking care of Preston," said Carmen.

"Oh, so she think she his momma now! That shit about to change," said Isabella.

After that phone call with Carmen, Isabella told her dad CJ, that her mother, his ex-wife, was dying. CJ took the news pretty bad.

"I'm gonna drive to Florida tomorrow to see your momma," said CJ.

"Why you gonna do that Dad? She don't want to see you," said Isabella.

"I needa ask ha ta forgive me. Tell ha I'm sorry fa what I did," said CJ.

"Momma not worried about you. I really do think she hates you," said Isabella.

"Nobody loved me like yo momma, so I know she don't hate me," said CJ.

Twenty

Mother of the Year

The very next morning CJ and Isabella drove to Florida to see Jo. When the two arrived at the hospital, they went up to the Intensive Care Unit, but the nurses would not let them in because visiting hours for the day hadn't begun.

"You are welcome to sit in the waiting room until visiting hours begin. Have a cup of coffee while you wait," said the nurse.

"But we're family," said Isabella. "Why can't we go back there now?"

"I'm sorry. It's hospital policy. Visiting hours do not begin until after shift change," the nurse answered.

Close to seven o'clock, Jaylynn walked into the waiting room. She had a rude awakening when she saw her dad and Isabella sitting in there.

"Where my son?" asked Isabella.

"YOUR son!" said Jaylynn.

"Yes, I am his momma. Not you!" said Isabella.

"A momma would know where her child is, so tell me what's wrong with this picture? Here you are asking me where your child is. Where have you been?" Jaylynn asked.

Isabella was speechless because she had no defense.

"Getting high right," said Jaylynn. "Just like you are at this very moment. Getting high has always been more important to you than anything else. Even your own son."

"MY son! You got that shit right. And he coming back to Miser with me," said Isabella.

"Now that's a lie. You'll have to kill me first," said Jaylynn.

"Stop ya'll," said CJ.

"Now you decide to be a daddy?" asked Jaylynn.

"Don't talk to him like that," Isabella said.

"Look, why don't both of you just leave. I don't know why you are even here. Especially you," said Jaylynn, as she looked at her dad, CJ. "Shouldn't you be with Candy?"

"He not with Candy no mo. She left him cuz he still love Momma," said Isabella.

"Oh really! I wish you could hear how stupid you sound. Get off the drugs Bell. Save the tiny little brain cells you might have left," Jaylynn said to her older sister.

"And look at yourself. Coming in here looking like who did and what for. All high! You have no respect."

"Fuck you!" Isabella snapped.

"You hear her Dad. She wants to fuck me just like that man was fucking you in the ass that night she saw you on all fours like a dog," said Jaylynn.

"Why you gotta go there?" asked Isabella.

"You brought me there," Jaylynn said to Isabella.

"We didn't come here to be judged by you, Little Girl" said Isabella.

"Then leave. Please leave, because this little girl who's been taking care of your son for the last two years of his life don't want or need your ass here. You're such a wonderful mother. When is the last time you've seen your son? Huh? How many birthdays has he had since you last saw him? And let's not talk about how wonderful of a daughter you are. You are such a good daughter, that you had to find out from someone else that your own mother is dying," said Jaylynn sarcastically.

"Shut up! We didn't come here to see you," said Isabella.

"You probably didn't come here to see Mom either. You're only here to see what you can get. That's it! You can't even wait until she's dead and cold," said Jaylynn.

"You shouldn't talk to yo sista like that," said CJ to Jaylynn.

"Why not? Just because you say not to!" asked Jaylynn. "You and Isabella are like two peas in a pod. Like father like daughter. Instead of trying to teach her better, you defend her heinous acts. But why should I expect any different from you? She is the way she is because of you and your no good ass family."

"Hello CJ. Isabella," Carmen interrupted as she walked into the waiting room.

"Hey Carmen," said CJ. "You don't wanna be in here. These girls been at it."

"What's going on Jay," asked Carmen.

"They came here to see Mom, but look at Bella. She's high and shit! She shouldn't be allowed to go back there to see Mom like that. She's so damn disrespectful!" Jaylynn said.

"Your mom wants to see her Jay. You know that. So just calm down and let her go back there," convinced Carmen.

"I guess you're going to tell me to let my dad go back there too," said Jaylynn.

"No. I am not going to tell you that. That's your call. Your mom asked me to make sure Isabella was informed, but she never said anything about CJ," Carmen answered.

Jaylynn looked at Isabella with hate in her eyes and said, "If it was up to me, you would never be able to see Mom again. You didn't respect her enough to consider her when she was alive and well, so I don't think you should be able to see her while she's sick and down."

While Jaylynn continued to talk to Isabella, she looked at her dad too and said, "The visiting block starts in five minutes. Bella, you can go back there to see Mom, because I know she has a mother's love for you. Dad, I will not allow you to see Mom, so I don't know why you came here."

Jo was asleep when Carmen and Isabella walked into the hospital room.

"Mom," said Isabella.

Jo opened her weak eyes, and when she saw Isabella standing there, her eyes opened wider with a quick sense of shock.

"What's wrong with her Carmen. Why is she looking like that?" asked Isabella.

"The doctors are giving her strong medication to keep her as comfortable as possible in these last stages," answered Carmen. "But she can understand you. Talk to her."

"I'm sorry for not being a good daughter, and I'm sorry for being a disappointment," said Isabella to Jo.

Jo was out of it that morning more so than usual, but she did make a few facial expressions indicating that she understood what Isabella was saying to her.

While Isabella was visiting with Jo, Jaylynn was still out in the waiting room with CJ.

"Why you so angry with me," CJ asked Jaylynn.

"Mom asked me not to be angry with you, so I have been trying with all I have to fight the feeling. But seeing you and Bella here this morning made those angry feelings resurface. Mom and I had a lot of time to talk these past couple of years. Is everything she told me about you and her relationship the truth? Did you really do all of those horrible things to her?" asked Jaylynn.

"As hard as it is fa me to admit, yo momma tode ya da trufth," said CJ. "I ain't have no daddy when I grew up, and my momma neva taught me betta. I ain't know hotta be a good daddy or husband."

"You were grown when you were with Mom. You were supposed to be a man. A real man protects his family. When anyone really loves someone, they automatically protect them," said Jaylynn. "Friends do that for one another, and you didn't even do that for us. We were your family."

CJ could not say anything to defend his past actions.

"The way I see it Dad, you never grew up, and you didn't deserve Mom. She was way too good for you," said Jaylynn.

Later that night Jo died peacefully in her sleep.

Twenty-One

Black Day

When Jo found out the severity of her illness, she took it upon herself to make her own funeral arrangements. She put her wishes in writing, and went over every single detail with Carmen and Jaylynn.

"I don't want the whole horse and pony show," said Jo. "I am not a fan of funerals with a bunch of people who haven't seen the deceased in years show up."

"But people will want to pay their respects," said Carmen.

"How can someone pay respects to me when I'm dead Carmen? I've never understood that," Jo said.

Carmen didn't know how to respond to Jo, because she herself was a social butterfly who loved being the center of attention. Even if it meant being center of attention after she was dead.

"Hear me out," said Jo. "Both of you know the people who are in and around my life on a regular basis. You know who I speak of and who I respect. Those are the people who mean something to me."

Jo told Carmen and Jaylynn that she wanted her body to be passed through the Catholic Church, and after, she wanted to be cremated.

"A small intimate funeral service would suffice," said Jo.

She made a list of approximately forty people who were always active in her life, and gave it to Carmen and Jaylynn.

"These people have been through life with me. They've been with me during my ups and downs. Stood by my side through every storm, and celebrated all of my accomplishments. If a person is not on this list, they're not or never have been an important part of my life, and there's no need for them to be at my funeral service. Can I trust you two to make sure of that?" asked Jo.

The two women nodded their heads at the same time.

When Carmen and Jaylyn made preparations for Jo's funeral service, they honored all of her wishes.

On the day of the funeral, Isabella arrived at the church with CJ. With them were CJ's mother, brother, and two sisters. The moment Carmen saw them walking up, she turned to Jaylynn and asked, "Do you want me to handle that?"

"No. I got this," answered Jaylynn as she walked slowly toward CJ and his family.

When Jaylynn approached them, one of CJ's sisters walked toward her and stretched out her arms to give Jaylynn a hug. When Jaylynn noticed that, she stopped in her tracks and gave a look that spoke loud enough to stop them all in their tracks.

"You people never cease to amaze me," said Jaylynn. "Please tell me you came to Florida on vacation and just so happen to be in the neighborhood."

"We came to show our respects," said CJ. "You think I neva loved yo momma, but you wrong."

"You had a funny way of showing it, just like now. Please leave and take that entourage of misfits with you," said Jaylynn.

"Did she just call us misfits?" asked CJ's older sister Pam.

"Yes I sure did, and if I wasn't at a church for my mother's funeral, I wouldn't be so nice," said Jaylynn.

CJ turned towards his family and said, "Ya'll go back to the car and wait."

"There's no need for them to wait. They need to leave and you need to go with them," said Jaylynn.

"You disrespectful. What they do to you? They yo family you talking to like that," said CJ.

"I am disrespectful, because I have no respect for them," said Jaylynn. "And you have the nerve to stand here and ask me that question like you are deaf, dumb, and blind. I can't believe you came here today after the conversation we had the other morning at the hospital. But then again, I can believe it."

"Jay, I know I got issues, but I loved yo momma. Let me go up and see ha this one last time," begged CJ.

When Jaylynn heard her dad's request, she looked him straight in the eyes and zoned off into deep thought. When she finally replied to him, she straightened her posture by standing upright with physical and mental strength evident.

"You're incapable of loving anyone, because love is nonexistent in your world. You may fool other people, but Mom saw the true you and I can see you too," said Jaylynn. "You should go, because as long as I am here, *Evil will not have the last look*."

Also by Açil Pichon

Evil In Front of You

Book One of the Stories of Jo Series

The True Essence of Evil

Book Two of the Stories of Jo Series

Visit us at: **www.acilpichon.com**

Printed in the United States of America